The Legend of the River Pumpkins

based on a true story

by Robert Klose

illustrations by Steve Klose

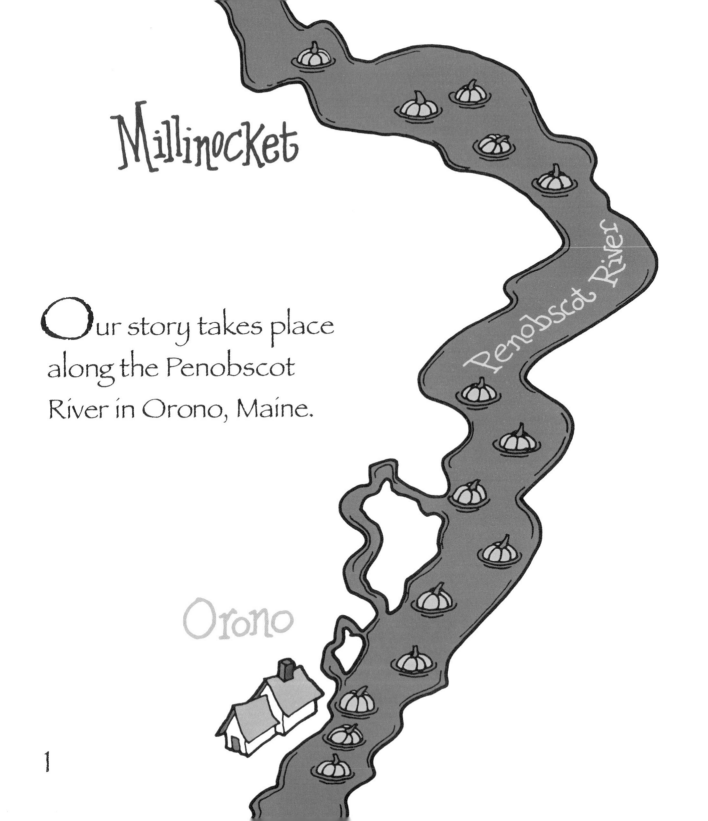

Millinocket

Our story takes place along the Penobscot River in Orono, Maine.

Penobscot River

Orono

1

The Legend of the River Pumpkins

based on a true story

2

There was once a man named Mr. Pinette who lived in a white house along the Penobscot River in the great state of Maine. A seven-year-old boy named Russell lived next door to him. The two were good friends and often went fishing together in the clear waters of the beautiful river.

It was autumn, and Halloween was fast approaching. The leaves in the trees were flame red and orange, the air was cool, and the wind whistled in the branches.

One morning Mr. Pinette wandered out of his house and down to the river. The water was calm and as still as a pond.

That's when he saw them. Bright orange spots standing out against the dark water. Mr. Pinette took a closer look.

Pumpkins.

In the Penobscot!

There must have been a dozen or so. Bobbing gently in a little cove along the riverbank, as if calling for attention.

Mr. Pinette smiled at the thought of river pumpkins and couldn't get them out of his head. How did they get there? Where had they come from? Had anybody ever heard of such a thing?

He asked all around town. Everybody shook their heads. Some even said, "Gosh, no! It's all news to us," and "River pumpkins? Impossible!"

Later that day, Mr. Pinette went down to the river again to see if the pumpkins were still there.

They were.

But there was something else. Russell, his hair as gold as the pumpkins were orange.

Mr. Pinette could see that Russell was crying, because he had his arms around himself and his shoulders were heaving. And every so often, if he listened carefully, he could hear Russell sob, "Oh, oh, oh!"

Mr. Pinette walked over to the boy. "What's the matter?" he asked, very quietly, so as not to startle him.

Russell turned. His tears had cut long, clean paths through his dusty cheeks. "It's almost Halloween," he sobbed. "And I don't have a pumpkin to carve into a jack o'lantern."

"So!" Mr. Pinette exclaimed, as he didn't know what else to say. And then he asked, "Why not?"

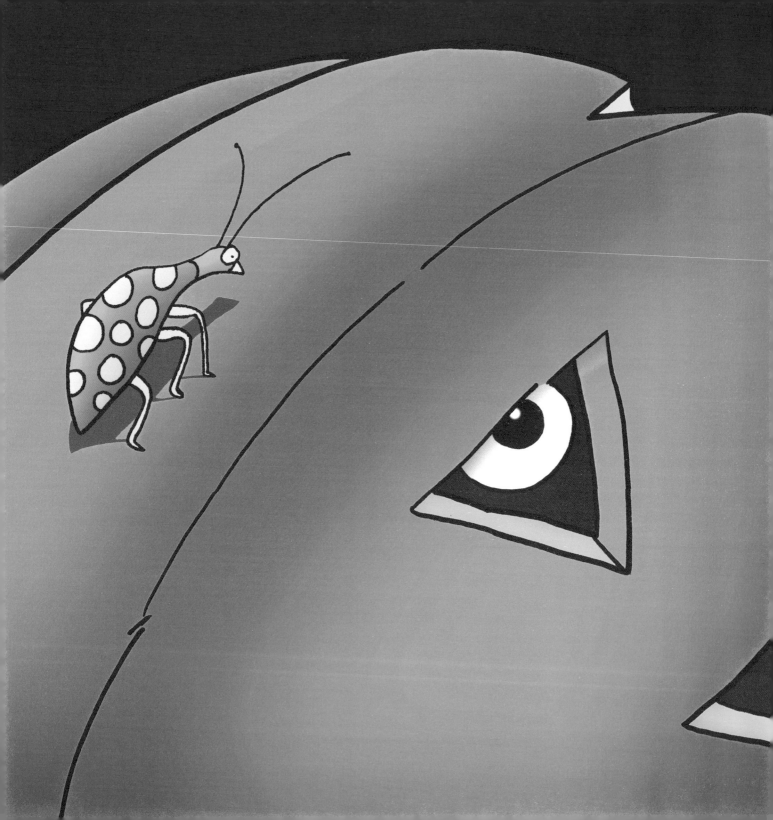

Russell sniffled and took a deep breath. Then he explained, "My mom says she's worried."

"Worried?" said Mr. Pinette.

"Yes, worried," said Russell. "She says pumpkins have bugs and goo."

"Bugs?"

"And goo," said Russell.

Mr. Pinette thought about this for a moment and then volunteered, "Well, maybe your mom will get unworried."

Russell shook his head. "Not before Halloween," he sniffed. "It takes her a long time to get unworried from things that worry her."

Maybe Russell's mom was right about the bugs and goo. But Mr. Pinette wondered if these were good enough reasons not to have a pumpkin for Halloween.

"Maybe she would let you have a pumpkin if you didn't carve it," he suggested. "You could just set it on the porch as it is."

Russell looked disappointed in Mr. Pinette's answer. "But then it wouldn't be a jack o'lantern," he said.

10

As Mr. Pinette stood with Russell his eyes wandered to the river. And then an idea jumped into his head.

"Russell," he said as he knelt down in front of the boy. "Your mom was talking about a regular old field pumpkin. But maybe she'll let you have a river pumpkin."

Russell made big eyes. He wiped his tears on his shirtsleeve. "Is there really such a thing?" he asked.

"Of course," said Mr. Pinette. "Look."

He turned Russell toward the cove in the river where the pumpkins were bobbing.

"It's true!" said Russell. "But where did they come from?"

Since nobody seemed to know where they came from, Mr. Pinette decided that it was up to him to take a guess.

"I've heard," he began, "that every year, way up north in Millinocket, the field pumpkins grow so big and plump that they break from their vines. Then they roll into the Penobscot River and float downstream to this very spot, for boys and girls to take for jack o'lanterns."

Russell smiled when he heard this story. And then Mr. Pinette said, "Are you ready?"

"For what?" Russell asked.

"To get your river pumpkin."

Russell clapped his hands and jumped in the air. Then he helped Mr. Pinette drag his canoe down the bank and into the river. After they were seated, they paddled out through the cool, dark water to the pumpkins.

"Take your pick," Mr. Pinette said, making a grand gesture with his arm. "Take any one you like."

While Mr. Pinette steadied the canoe, Russell reached over the side and grabbed the biggest pumpkin. He pulled and strained and huffed until he had tumbled it into the boat.

It landed with a thud.

Then they paddled back to shore.

Mr. Pinette watched as Russell got out of the canoe and grabbed hold of his pumpkin. It was so big that he could barely get his arms around it. As Mr. Pinette tied up the canoe Russell made his way up the river bank. He swayed this way and that as he carried the tremendous pumpkin.

He headed straight for his house.

Mr. Pinette followed at a short distance, until he heard the front door open. "Russell!" cried the boy's mom. "That pumpkin is dripping wet."

Still holding the pumpkin, Russell swallowed hard. At first he could barely speak. And then he found the right words. "It's a river pumpkin!" he announced.

"Hmmm," said his mom, putting a hand to her chin. "Does it have any bugs?"

"Not that I know," said Russell, and he began to explain.

"Every year, up in Millinocket, the field pumpkins get big and fat and break from their vines and roll into the river.

"Then they float down here for boys and girls to take for jack o'lanterns."

Russell's mom rolled her eyes. "What a story!" she said. "I've never heard such a thing in my life!"

Mr. Pinette saw that Russell was now worried that he might lose his river pumpkin. Russell's legs began to shake. His knees began to knock. His shoulders began to heave. And all the while he clutched his gigantic pumpkin for dear life.

Mr. Pinette knew it was time to make his move. He came up right behind Russell and greeted his mother. "Hello, Mrs. Osnoe," he said. And then he looked down at her little boy, trembling under the weight of his enormous pumpkin.

"Hey, Russell," he said. "That's a mighty fine river pumpkin you have there. Mighty fine!"

Mrs. Osnoe's eyebrows flew up. "Whaaat?" she said. "Then it's true?"

"Oh, yes," said Mr. Pinette. And then he explained. "Every year, up in Millinocket, the field pumpkins grow so big and plump that they break from their vines. Then they tumble into the river and travel downstream to this very spot, for boys and girls to take for jack o'lanterns." After a pause he added, "Just in time for Halloween."

Mrs. Osnoe just stood there, staring at Mr. Pinette. Then, without a word, she stepped aside. Russell stumbled into the house, where he was finally able to put down his big, fat, heavy pumpkin.

Hours passed. The sun went down. The moon and stars came out. And that very evening, on Russell's porch, there was an immense jack o'lantern. The biggest on the block.

It was smiling.

And it had stories to tell.

12230671R00013

Made in the USA
Charleston, SC
21 April 2012